VANESSA'S ROTTEN DAY

enjoy, ♡
Collette

A whimsical tale based on a true animal rescue story

Written by
Collette Treewater and Roberta R. Carr
Illustrated by Debora Strand

ISBN 13: 978-1533629357
ISBN-10: 1533629358

Printed in the United States

Dedicated to animal healers everywhere

Hello there! My name is Vanessa. I'm a kid like you except for one tiny detail. You are a person, and I am a turkey vulture. No big deal, right?

What?!?

Did you say vultures SCARE you? Oh, please say it isn't so!

Perhaps if I share a few things about myself, you won't be frightened. Who knows? Once you get to know me, we might even become friends.

Shall I begin by describing my beautiful red head? It is small compared to the rest of my body, but that doesn't mean I have a dinky brain. Actually, I'm pretty smart. My wing tips are shaped like long feathered fingers, and I have flat, chicken-like feet.

You've probably spotted me circling high in the sky over fields and freeways. You may also have seen me hanging out by the side of a road. Usually, I am searching for my next meal. Some people call us scavengers, but I prefer the term, *Hungry Hunters*. The name has a catchy ring to it, don't you agree?

Speaking of food, I eat dead animals. When an unlucky squirrel, raccoon or deer gets smashed by a car, it's my job to clean up the mess. This probably sounds icky to you, but it's my purpose in life. If you think about it, vultures provide a valuable service. Do you want smelly critters lying all over the place? Of course not! You will be pleased to know I make them disappear.

Would it surprise you to learn vultures are shy? I try not

to bother people, but if you and I accidentally meet on a hiking trail, I may hiss or grunt. This is how I talk, so don't freak out. My voice sounds harsh, as though I am mad or something, but I'm not. It's just me being me.

Whatever you do, NEVER startle me. You know, sneak up from behind and shout 'Boo!' If I feel threatened, I may barf on you. Seriously! I don't have sharp talons like other birds, so this is how I defend myself. You should know my vomit smells REALLY bad. Kind of like stinky dog poop—only SO much worse. Trust me, you don't want to be anywhere near it.

I could go on and on, but I'm guessing you would rather read an exciting story than learn more facts. Well, wait no more. I have a story that will knock your socks off. After hearing it, you may even say, "That could NEVER happen! No way! Not in a MILLION years!"

But it did happen. I know because it happened to ME. The authors may have exaggerated a few things, but the truth is I had a very rotten day and lived to tell about it. It's time to sit back, relax, and pay attention. You won't believe what you are about to learn.

Your new friend,
Vanessa T. Vulture

No Fair!

The story begins late one August afternoon when my twin brother, Jason, arrives home, plops down in our field, and shouts at the top of his lungs, "GUESS WHAT I FOUND TODAY?"

Everyone stops what they are doing and stares at him.

"Gather around, and I'll tell you about it."

My brother loves being the center of attention. Usually I ignore him, but today he sounds extra excited. Even I am curious about what he has to say. Uncle Kenny jumps down from our roosting tree first. Others soon follow, and before long, all of us are huddled around Jason, anxiously awaiting the big news.

"While hunting today, I found a dead seal near Muir Woods." He smiles proudly. "And four rotting fish. I had a tasty lunch, but there is plenty left for you." Jason pauses to let his words sink in. "Want me to take you there?"

"Great discovery, son," our dad says while glancing at the sunset. "How about leading us there tomorrow? For breakfast." Daddy wraps his wing around Jason's shoulder. "It's a little late to fly there now."

"Fine with me," Jason says happily.

I enjoy hearing about the food. I mean, who wouldn't want to chew on a tasty seal or nibble on slimy fish? But that is not what interests me. Muir Woods is a special place, and I have never seen it. I hop next to Jason and whisper in his ear, "Will you tell me about the trees? Do they really touch the sky?"

"The redwoods are amazing, little sister. One day, I'll take you there"—he playfully taps my head with his wingtip—"when you are ready."

I push him away. I do not like being teased—especially in front of everyone. Jason acts as if he is better than me, and it makes me MAD. Boiling mad, like hot, steamy water whistling from a teakettle.

More than anything, I

want to see those giant redwoods. But my parents won't let me. They say I'm not strong enough to fly there and back. But I am strong! I'm ready! I KNOW I can do it! *Why won't my parents trust me like they trust Jason?*

NO FAIR!

Taking Care of Rosie

The next morning, my family and I perch on branches with our wings spread wide, swaying like kites in a breeze. We do this because our feathers get wet at night. The sun, our friend, dries them so we can fly safely.

Once my wings are ready, I smooth out the heart-shaped necklace that hangs around my neck. I found it on the ground while hunting one day, and it was love at first sight. I notice Daddy watching, so I flap my wings wildly, causing leaves on the tree to shimmy. I want him to see my strength so he will take me to Muir Woods today.

Jason snickers and shakes his head. "Nice try, little sister, but no deal. You still can't come with us."

My brother CANNOT tell me what to do! He is NOT the boss! I stomp a foot in protest, and start falling off the branch, but Daddy catches me just in time. *Whew! That was a close one.*

Jason snickers again, which makes my nostrils flare.

Momma speaks in a calming voice, "You are almost ready to fly longer distances, Vanessa. But we want you to be safe."

"Aw, Mom! I'm ready NOW! I can do this! Please let me go!" I beg, hoping she changes her mind. But she doesn't budge. Not one inch.

Momma tips her head toward my younger cousin. "Besides, Rosie needs company. You can take care of her while we are gone."

I glance at Rosie. Yesterday, she crashed into a tree and became dizzy. Her mom won't let her fly right now so she's stuck at home.

Momma hugs me. "Please be a good girl and do what I ask."

I fold my wings and grunt loudly. *I don't want to stay with Rosie! I want to fly to Muir Woods with everyone else! No fair!*

. . . .

Jason steps next to Momma. "The air is perfect for flying. We should go." He tries tapping my head again, but I pull back. No way is he touching me. He shrugs, jumps off a branch, and climbs into the sky. "Follow the leader!" he yells to everyone except Rosie and me.

Momma bounces her legs a few times, then leaps gracefully into the air. She swoops past and says, "Remember...take care of Rosie," before joining Jason on their great adventure.

The rest of the family spread their wings and begin leaping out of the tree. One...two...three, four, five, six, seven, and finally, eight. They tip their wings from side-to-side as they soar away on warm pockets of air.

After everyone disappears into the distance, I glance at

Rosie. She immediately sticks out her tongue. "Let's play tag. You're it!"

I sigh loudly. Today is going to be a long and BORING day.

The Decision

After playing tag, Rosie and I sit down to rest. A gurgling sound, like water in a clogged drain, fills the air. We look at each other and giggle at the same time.

"Was that your tummy?" I ask her.

She nods. "Guess I'm hungry. I need some grub."

I search for our family, but only see miles of blue sky. No vultures anywhere. "Momma said to stay home, Rosie." I try my best to comfort her, "We'll eat after everyone returns. It shouldn't be too much longer."

"But I'm hungry now," Rosie cries. "You heard my stomach growl. Can you find food for me? Just a snack?"

Rosie knows Momma said not to go anywhere. I remind her of this fact for a second time.

But my cousin doesn't let up, not even for a second. "Please, Vanessa! I'm starving! You PROMISED to take care of me. Remember?"

Rosie acts dramatic at times. I think she wants to be an actress when she grows up. Who knows? Maybe she will work on *Animal Planet* and become a superstar.

But Momma did put me in charge. *Isn't making decisions a part of that responsibility?* Perhaps I can find food nearby so Rosie doesn't have to suffer. I sniff the air for a dead raccoon or deer or rabbit.

No odors. No scents. Nothing. Suddenly, my stomach gurgles, too.

"I can't wait any longer!" Rosie cries louder. "I need food NOW! Or I'll faint!" She presses her wings together as if she's begging. "PLEASE, Vanessa!"

Although I want to ignore her whining, letting Rosie go hungry seems unkind. Especially when I can do something about it.

"Will you promise to stay home? I mean it, Rosie. You can't follow. Your mom said NO flying."

Her eyes grow as big as cupcakes. "Does this mean…"

"Yes, I will hunt. But you stay put."

"I will! I will! Cross my heart! Thank you, Vanessa!"

Rosie bounces up and down real fast like a kid on a trampoline. "You're the best cousin in the whole world!"

While she shrieks and carries on, an idea fills my brain. Maybe—just maybe—if my family sees how well I take care of her, they will let me fly to Muir Woods. They will see how responsible I am. This seems like a perfect way to prove myself.

"I better find you here when I return." We stand so close that our noses touch. "No goofing around, Rosie. Got it?"

She hisses loudly, which means 'Sure thing!' in vulture talk.

I move to a high branch like Daddy taught me. When a warm gust arrives, I leap into the air, hold out my wings, and fan my tail. The wind lifts me into the sky. I glance at Rosie to make sure she has not followed.

"Thank you!" she yells, waving from the ground. "I'll be waiting!"

Once in the air, I almost forget about my annoying cousin. Oh, how I love to fly! Soaring over Novato is so much fun. It's a country town with lots of open space, and I enjoy watching all the action below. A herd of thirsty cows parade toward a water barrel to get a drink. Two ladies walk along a trail while their dogs chase lizards and rabbits into the bushes. A group of men and women aim their binoculars toward a pair of western bluebirds that are perched in a tree.

The search for breakfast takes me further away from home, and I begin to worry. A voice inside my head shouts, *'You are disobeying your parents. Return home now!'* I remind myself that Rosie is hungry and cannot fly. She needs my help. I keep searching for food, hoping it is the right decision.

Rotten Luck

I rock my wings and sway through the air, scanning for food, but don't see any. When I arrive at my family's favorite hunting area, I tip my wing and drop closer to the ground. It's a cool hunting trick Momma taught me.

I swoop across a farm, and FINALLY catch a whiff of something good. I drop lower and smell a gas released by dead animals. My hunt takes me to a large black and white dog that is half-buried in the soil between two tall oak trees. An old farmhouse and red barn appear in the distance.

Score! It's chow time for Rosie and me.

I land next to the dog. The poor thing looks like she has been dead for a while. Her fur is matted with mud, and flies are buzzing over her body. I glance around to make sure I am alone. I don't want to become a coyote's breakfast if you know what I mean.

The coast is clear, so I hop on top of the dog, causing the flies to scurry away. I take my first bite. *Yummy!* The dog tastes delicious, like a juicy cheeseburger with lettuce and tomato.

Here is another fun fact. I have a pouch inside my neck that is called a crop. I cannot carry food with my beak or feet, but I can store it in my crop. When I return home, I will cough up the dog meat for Rosie to eat. This may sound gross to you, but it's how vultures feed babies and injured cousins.

I eat until I am stuffed. A nap sounds mighty nice, but Rosie is waiting for breakfast, so I take off to fly home. I feel super proud for taking care of my younger cousin. Everything is going according to plan.

Then something unexpected happens.

Crash Landing

My tummy begins to hurt. A sick type of hurt. Not the 'I'm full' kind. Not the 'I've got the flu' kind. It's the type of pain that occurs after eating five brownies, a large pepperoni pizza, and three bowls of buttered popcorn in one sitting.

My wings feel like they weigh a hundred pounds, and I zigzag all over the place. I fall toward the ground. Faster... faster... faster...

I search for a safe place to land, but can only see neighborhoods filled with houses, people, and cars. No open fields. No good place for a vulture.

Luckily, I spot an older man and a little girl working in a

backyard. The girl tosses seeds on the ground for hungry doves, while the man fills a hummingbird feeder. This yard of bird-lovers has to be a safe place to land, right?

I hope so because I am going down…down…down…

I crash to the earth. *Splat!* My head spins. My wings won't move. My chest aches, and I can barely breathe. My legs flop around like cooked spaghetti.

My body trembles as a human shadow slowly closes in. I have never been more scared in my life.

I want my mother!

Emergency 911!

My head pounds like ten drummers drumming, but I try not to panic. *Perhaps this is a bad dream. When I wake up, I will be safe at home with Rosie.*

But it is not a dream.

I blink, and notice the girl sitting cross-legged beside me. A human has never been this close. *Will she harm me?*

"Papa! Come quick!" the girl suddenly shouts. "You won't believe what I found!"

She touches my back feathers, but jerks her hand away like she has touched fire. "Papa! We have a BIG problem!"

A man wearing a Greek Fisherman's hat soon arrives. He tilts his head while watching me with a curious expression.

"What is it, Papa?"

"Well, Ruby"—he hovers over me—"you are looking at a young turkey vulture. A very sick one."

Oh happy day! The man knows I'm a vulture. He speaks in a caring way, and seems smart. I bet he can—

All of a sudden, my stomach rumbles like a volcano. White foam oozes out of my mouth and dribbles on the ground.

"Oh, no!" Ruby squeals in a panicky voice. "What's wrong with her?"

"I don't know," Papa says. "But she needs help."

"What should we do?"

Papa removes a phone from his pocket. "I know who to call."

. . . .

Time passes, and I lie there unable to move. My eyes burn, and my stomach aches. Ruby touches my feathers again, but this time she doesn't pull away. Instead, she runs her fingers gently down my back. "Papa, did you know vultures have purple feathers?"

"They're not really purple, Ruby. It's more like a purple sheen on brownish black feathers. The shiny color comes from reflected light. Vultures look different close up, don't they?"

"Uh-huh. I didn't know—"

A truck screeches to a halt in front of the house, interrupting their conversation. A woman dressed in brown shorts hurries into the yard, carrying a box with holes punched in both sides.

"Did you call the Humane Society about an injured vulture?" she asks Papa.

"I did." He motions toward me.

The woman sets the box on the ground and kneels down beside me.

"She seems awfully sick," Papa says. "I think we might lose her."

What?!? You can't LOSE me. I'm right here!

"I'll take her to a wildlife hospital," the woman says. "They'll know what to do."

The woman reaches down, scoops me up, and stuffs me into the box. I try to stand, but can't move. Not my head, not my mouth, not my body. Only my mind works.

"I'm worried, Papa," Ruby says. "Will she be all right?"

"I'll take good care of her," the woman says.

After writing Papa's name and phone number in a book, she carries me to her truck. She opens a side door, and carefully slides my box inside. Once the door closes, the blue sky and warm winds disappear, and I am left alone in the dark as the truck drives away.

What will happen to me?

Racing to the Hospital

The lady drives through streets and onto a freeway, tossing me around like it's a windy day. Each mile takes me further away from home. *Will I ever see my family again?*

We come to a screeching halt. The lady opens the door and slides me out. "Let's get you inside. Amy is a great vet. She'll know what to do."

. . . .

The truck lady steps inside a building and rushes down a hallway. She plunks me on a table. "Hey, everyone. Here's the vulture I called about."

Several humans gather around and begin chattering.

"That's one sick bird," a man says.

"Is she breathing?" a brown-haired woman asks.

"She's barely alive," the truck lady cautions. "You need to act fast."

It is eerie hav-ing everyone talk about me as if I'm not here. I want to scream, *'I can hear you!'* but I'm too weak. It takes all of my energy to keep my brain working.

Two strong

hands lift me out of the box. My head and neck dangle like a wet noodle, and before long, I am lying on a hard table.

A woman wearing a mask and blue gloves shines a light into my eyes, temporarily blinding me. "What's going on with you, little vulture?" She takes a gadget from around her neck and inserts tips into her ears. She presses a flat end to my chest and listens. "Faint heartbeat," she mutters. She flashes light into my eyes again, and touches me here and there, mumbling something about not finding reflexes.

"What'd you think, Amy?" the truck lady says to the woman who is examining me. "Will she survive?"

"Her eyes are dilated and fixed. Not good. We'll do what we can. Let's hope she's a fighter."

No reflexes? Eyes dilated? What the heck does that mean? I wish Amy the vet used words I understood.

The truck lady sets a paper on the counter. "I'll get out of your way. Good luck with her."

Amy looks up. "Thanks for bringing her in so quickly."

"No problem. I hope she makes it."

The Miracle Workers

People scurry in and out of the crowded room, and I lose track of time. Someone asks, "Was she poisoned?"

"I'd bet money on it." Amy looks at her helpers and says, "You know the drill, folks. Let's begin."

A man stands at the end of the table and holds my head firmly in his hands. A woman gives Amy a long silver tool that looks like scissors except it has curved ends instead of pointy ones. Suddenly, Amy forces my beak open and plunges that thing down my throat.

WHAT IS SHE DOING?!?

Amy presses on my crop with one hand while poking around inside of my throat with that metal tool. I gag as she

removes bits of food.

"That stuff smells disgusting!" a man says while pinching his nose.

Amy ignores the comment and keeps working. She forces that silver thing down my throat a second time, reaching and grabbing for who knows what. *I can't take anymore! Help me! STOP helping! I don't know what I want.*

Amy pulls out several chunks of meat and gets super excited. "Oh, good! Undigested food." She drops a piece of meat in a jar and tells a man, "Please send this to the lab for analysis." Amy relaxes and breathes a little easier.

I relax, too, now that Amy is done. *Whew! I'm glad that's over.*

Amy presses her shoulders back. "Ready to flush her out?" she asks her helpers.

What?!? Does that mean—

The man grips my body tighter and holds me in place while Amy inserts a tiny tube in my nose. Then she slides a larger tube all the way down my throat. She connects that tube to a water bag and fills my tummy, turning me into a giant water balloon.

Yikes! Are they trying to drown me? I want to stop them, but cannot move or speak. I am about to burst when Amy removes the tube from my throat. She nods at the man, and he quickly flips me upside down! I'm not joking! My feet are up, my head is down. It's crazy!

Before long, water and food come flowing out of my mouth. I am dizzy, choking, and tired. I don't know how much more I can take.

After emptying my stomach, the man swings me upright, making my head whirl. Meanwhile, Amy is holding a thin plastic tube with a long needle. Someone covers my head with a towel, and pain suddenly rips through my body.

Wowza! Did she just poke me?

The towel slips away as Amy fills a second tube with white liquid. *Ouch!* A second jab.

"If it's rat poison, Vitamin K should help," Amy says, removing her mask and gloves, and wiping sweat from her forehead. "Well done, folks. Let's move our patient to an incubator. She needs to rest."

The man gently lays me inside a glass container, which is only slightly bigger than my body. Once he snaps the lid shut, Amy presses a button and air flows into the space, which makes breathing easier.

I have never been locked up, not once in my life. I cannot move. I cannot talk. I cannot do anything. Even my mind is fading.

The cold room causes me to shiver. Scary noises—moans, wails and howls—
fill the air. It sounds
spooky, like visiting
a haunted house on
Halloween.

I'm about ready
to give up when Amy
fastens a lamp to a
pole and rolls it next
to my cage. She flips
on a switch, causing a
dim red light to blan-

ket my body. The warmth comforts me, like snuggling between Momma and Daddy on a cold rainy night.

Amy watches for a long time. She eventually whispers, "We've done all we can, little vulture. The rest is up to you." She covers my cage with a towel and leaves the room.

I am weak, exhausted, and all alone in this strange place. Tears roll down my face as everything goes dark.

Poor Little Vulture

I wake up, not knowing whether it is day or night, up or down. My body feels like someone has used it for a punching bag. I have aches and pains everywhere. My throat is raw. I try lifting my head, but cannot move it.

A door swings open and a woman strolls into the room. She watches me for a few minutes while shaking her head. "Poor little vulture," she mumbles. "Guess it wasn't meant to be." She releases a sad sigh before walking away.

Why did she call me a 'poor little vulture'? I have more questions, but my head throbs so I drift back to sleep.

. . . .

The click of a door awakens me. Amy walks in and lifts the top of my cage. She listens to my heart, and shines that dreadful light into my eyes again. I want to yell, *'Turn that thing off!'* but no sound comes out. My body lies there like a sack of potatoes.

"Eyes still dilated," Amy mutters. "I think we might lose you."

Here we go again. Helloooo! I'm right here!

A lady walks over and asks Amy, "What's next?"

"I'll give her more fluids"—Amy shakes her head—"but that's it. There's nothing else we can do." She fills a tube with water and pokes a needle under my skin. This time I barely feel the pinch. Afterward, she whispers, "Fight, 1474. Fight with all your might."

I briefly wonder what 1474 means, but decide it doesn't matter. I have no energy for anything—especially to fight. I am ready to give up when images of Momma, Daddy, and Jason magically appear in my mind. They must be terribly worried.

Thinking about my family gives me a ray of hope. In this moment, I make three promises to myself: I WILL fight hard. I WILL get better. I WILL see my family again. I am NOT giving up.

My brain hurts from all this thinking, so I switch it off and sleep.

The Road to Recovery

Amy listens to my heart and shines that light into my eyes so often I lose count. I know she cares by how often she visits, so I cooperate. I make no fuss when she examines me. I sip water, but it is hard to swallow. I focus on breathing: in, out, in, out. I am not giving up.

By the second or third day—I can't remember—I finally lift my head. I do it a few times, like lifting weights: One, two. One, two. One, two. It may not sound like much, but it is a BIG deal.

And check this out. Later in the day, something amazing happens. I push my body up and stand on my legs for THREE whole seconds!

Can you believe it?

When Amy visits, I have a surprise for her. I lie quietly,

waiting for the perfect moment. Just as she opens the top of my cage, I raise my head and whisper, "Hiss, hiss. *Hello, Amy.*"

She gasps while stepping back. "I don't believe it! You have a voice!"

I clear my throat and introduce myself. "Hiss, hiss, hiss. *My name is Vanessa.*"

Amy's eyes get big and glossy like a Beanie Boos Muffin Cat. She steps back and shouts, "Hey guys! Come here and check this out!"

A bunch of people huddle around the table.

If talking impresses them, wait until they see my next trick. I steady myself and slowly stand. Ta-Daa! Everyone claps and cheers.

"Will you look at that?" Amy gushes.

"Hiss, hiss, hiss, grunt, grunt. *Thanks for taking care of me.*"

"She's so strong!" a man declares. "Standing and talking. Incredible!"

"This patient no longer needs an incubator," a woman says while motioning toward the hallway. "I'll get a cage ready for her in the other room."

Amy nods. "I agree. She's on her way to recovery."

Poison

The next morning, I check out my new cage. It's larger than the first one, and has thick metal bars instead of glass windows. I am still locked up, but at least I can move around.

A door squeaks open. Amy walks in, unlocks my cage, and pokes my body here and there. Afterward, she sits on a chair and scribbles in a notebook.

Why she isn't talking? Did I do something wrong?

She sets her pen down and walks away, but returns a few minutes later. She opens my cage, pours fresh water in a bowl, and tosses in two dead mice. She locks the door and writes in her book again.

I sniff the food, but don't want to eat. I would rather chat with Amy. Last night, I practiced several new words and want to share them with her. I clear my throat, "Hiss, hiss, hisssss, grunt. *You are beautiful, Amy.*"

Her head pops up. "Nice! Those are healthy sounds." She stares at me while biting the tip of her pen. Finally she says, "Want to hear my plans for you?"

Zip-a-Dee-Doo-Dah! She's talking again!

I settle down in the front of the cage to give her my full attention.

"It's time to rebuild your strength. You need to flap your wings. Get ready. I'm busting you out of here in a few days."

Before Amy can explain what she means, a lady walks in, waving a piece of paper. "I have lab results."

Amy tilts her head toward me. "For 1474?"

The lady nods, frowning. "You were right. She was poisoned. But not from rats. She probably ate a farm animal. One that was put to sleep by its owner."

"Darn! I was afraid of that."

The lady hands a paper to Amy and leaves the room. Amy studies it in silence for a long time. All of a sudden she rants, "Grrrr…it's so frustrating not knowing what she ate before getting sick…that's the second patient in a month…how many more wild animals will get sick before we figure this out? Grrr…"

Poor Amy. She looks unhappy. But I know how to fix it. I can tell her about my last meal.

"Hiss, grunt! Hiss, hiss, hiss, hiss! *Good news! I can show you the dog!*"

Amy shakes her head and chuckles. "You're sure a lively one." She files the lab report in the back of her book and leaves.

I guess the dog conversation will have to wait for another time.

A Temporary Home

Several days later, Amy tucks me inside a smaller cage and walks through the hospital. When she opens an outside door, a blast of sunlight makes my eyes squint. Blue sky, white puffy clouds, and fresh air greet us. *Ahhh...* I breathe in the sweet scents of nature.

Amy strolls through a courtyard where various animals are caged. A falcon with one eye, an owl with a damaged foot, and an older vulture all stare as we pass by. A Snowy Egret squawks at us from a rooftop perch. They seem as curious about me as I am about them.

Amy steps toward a fence, opens a gate, and enters a private area. The door slams shut, blocking out the other animals. *Why can't I stay with them? Especially the vulture. We could keep each other company.*

We stop in front of a large cage. It's the size of a kid's bedroom, and has wire mesh walls with a tall ceiling. Grass and bushes grow in a dirt floor. Several perches—swings, fences, tree branches—are positioned in various places. A water bowl sits in a corner.

"Welcome to the flight aviary." Amy nudges me inside. "I hope you enjoy your new digs."

I hop through the gate, but trip over my big feet. *Plop!* I tumble to the ground and bump my nose.

"You OK?" Amy helps me up. "Looks like you have some work to do before I take you home."

Did she say home? As in my REAL home?

"You must eat and exercise to rebuild your strength."

Just then, the gate squeaks open. A man arrives and sets a silver bowl in front of me. "Amy found this dead raccoon by the side of the road this morning. She saved it for you." He nudges me toward it. "Go ahead. Eat some. You'll like it."

I check out the room service. *Sniff, sniff.* I tear off a small chunk of meat and gobble it down. *Umm, umm, good!* I take a second bite.

"Good girl," Amy says happily. "Enjoy your condo." She and the man leave.

Amy's condo comment is funny. It's only a big birdcage, but I love her sense of humor.

After finishing lunch, I sit back, relax, and let my mind drift. I am lucky to be alive after getting sick. I am thankful to the man and girl who helped me after I crashed in their back-yard. I appreciate the woman from the Humane Society who

drove me here. I don't know what I would have done without Amy and her helpers. They saved my life.

But I desperately miss my family.

I decide to work hard to get healthy for two reasons. First, I want to return home to see Momma, Daddy, and Jason. Second, I keep thinking about the words 'last meal' and 'poison.' I must find a way to tell Amy about that dog before another vulture eats it and gets sick.

Friendships are Important

Every day I follow the same routine. Drink water. Eat food.
Flap my wings. Jump back and forth from the ground to perches.
I do everything Amy asks, but I am still here. I want to be free,
not locked inside a big cage. I am lonely and want to be with
my family.

One evening after the visitors leave, I call out to the
vulture who lives on the other side of the fence. Maybe he is
lonely, too, and would like to talk.

He returns my hisses right away and says his name is
Freddie. I learn many interesting things about him. For ex-
ample, a man stole him from a nest when he was a baby and
raised him as a pet. Now, he actually prefers living in a cage and
hanging out with humans, rather than living in the wild with
other vultures.

Freddie tells his story calmly, not sounding upset about what happened to him. I don't know if I could be that forgiving. Anyway, he seems like a nice fellow, so I ask about some strange noises on his side of the fence today. I describe the yells, screams, and squeals that rattled my nerves. The uproar sounded like a pack of hungry wolves, growling and searching for food.

Freddie chuckles before explaining what happened. As an ambassador for the hospital, it is his job to teach visitors about vultures. But sometimes he likes to have a little fun. Today, a spunky five-year-old girl with curly blonde hair and sparkly blue eyes smiled at him. He decided to perform his famous hip-hop dance for her and her friends. He flew from a perch, to the ground, and then spun around super fast in a circle. The noise I heard came from a group of children who were laughing, clapping, and having a good time.

Phew! That's welcome news.

I thank Freddie for the explanation. I ask if he ever wants to live in the wild. I describe my wonderful family and invite him to stay with us. He says no; it is too late for him to change. He is an old vulture, and likes living here with the other ambassadors.

I silently pray it isn't too late for me. Although the humans are kind, I want the freedom to soar over hills and valleys. I want to roost with my family in our special tree. I want to hunt for my own food, and to visit places like Muir Woods. I want to go home.

. . . .

After Freddie and I finish talking, the gate swings open.

Amy arrives for an evening visit. "Did you have a good day, 1474?" she asks, while biting into a juicy red apple.

One of Freddie's visitors used an interesting word today. I think Amy will like it so I take a deep breath and let it rip, "Hissssssssssssssssssssssssssss! *Supercalifragilisticexpialidocious!*"

Amy drops her head back and laughs out loud. A fun-loving, wild kind of roar. "Someone is feisty tonight." She takes another bite of apple. "Keep up the good work. You'll be home in no time."

"Hiss? Hiss, grunt? *Really? You promise?*"

"Can you keep a secret?" Amy whispers. "You and I aren't supposed to talk with each other. You know, act as if we are friends."

She drags a hose to my water bowl. "That's why I call you 1474. Your patient number is less personal." She fills my bowl with fresh water.

Her words leave me speechless. *Why can't we be friends? Or talk to each other? Is it because of what happened to Freddie?*

"But I'm breaking the rules for you," Amy continues talking while curling up the hose. "This hospital treats thousands of animals each year, and I've never met a talker quite like you. You're different from the rest." She smiles. "I will miss our daily chats."

Amy flings the apple core into a trashcan. "Well, it's been a long day, and I need to go home and get some sleep." She locks up for the night. "Pleasant dreams, little girl. See you tomorrow."

After the gate closes, I think about Amy's words for a long time. On one hand, I understand why she needs to keep a distance from her patients. She wants us to return to the wild, not get comfortable here. Animals like Freddie and the falcon with one eye have no choice. They probably would not survive in nature. That's why she keeps us separated. I get how things work.

But friendships are important. I mean, where would I be without the nice man and little girl, the truck lady and Amy? These humans saved my life. They are my friends now. Nothing anyone can say will ever change my mind.

Problem Solving

A few days later, Amy and a lady stand by my cage, chatting back and forth. I hop closer to eavesdrop on their conversation.

"I wish we knew what poisoned the vulture," the lady says. "I don't want her to get sick again after she leaves here."

"You and me both," Amy replies. "It's frustrating not knowing what she ate for her last meal in the wild. That clue might lead us to the poison."

"Hiss, hiss, hiss, grunt, GRUNT! Grunt, hiss, hiss. *I ate a black and white DOG! I can take you to it!*"

Amy raises an eyebrow and says, "What's got you all worked up?"

I pace back and forth, feeling frustrated. I need to find a better way to communicate with her. I hop next to a map of Marin County hanging on the wall, find Mount Burdell, and begin pecking.

Amy walks closer. "What are you doing?"

Peck, peck, peck…

The other lady joins us. "What's going on with 1474?"

"I'm not sure," Amy says, grinning. "Maybe she likes playing with maps."

"Hiss, hiss! *Very funny.* Hiss, hiss. Hiss, grunt, grunt? *Come closer. What do you see?*" I peck five more times, creating a hole in the paper.

"She keeps striking the same spot," the lady says. "I wonder what it means?"

Amy rests her hand on her chin as she studies the map. "She's pecking at Mount Burdell."

"Hiss, hiss, grunt! *Way to go, Amy!*" I know if we drive in that direction, we will pass the farm and I can show her the dog. I stop pecking, stand back, and relax.

"You like Mount Burdell?" Amy squats next to the map. "You want to be released there?"

"Hiss, hiss, hiss! *Now we're talkin'!*" I hop on a perch and fan my wings like I'm ready to fly home.

"Well, I guess that settles it," Amy says. "I'll take you to your favorite Novato mountain in the morning."

Yipeeee! I can hardly believe my ears. I bounce up and down, but lose energy when Amy and I lock eyes. Something passes between us—a moment of sadness. I rub my head against her soft hand, the hand that saved my life. "Hiss, hiss, hiss, grunt. *I will never forget you.*"

"Wow. What just happened?" the lady asks, shaking her head. "I've never seen a vulture do that before. Not once in the six years I've worked here."

"I know what you mean." Amy winks at me. "She's a special one."

The woman gives Amy a thumbs-up, and leaves the aviary. Amy writes in a notebook for a few minutes, then leaves for the night.

My pulse races with excitement. I am going home. *Hip, hip, hurray!*

I visualize my family roosting in our hollow tree. I can't wait to hug everyone. Then I think about that last meal and the word 'poison' again.

I must find a way to show Amy the dog before she takes me home. But how?

Communicating with Humans

I wake up the next morning feeling on top of the world. Today is the big day. I am going home. Amy arrives early to organize everything. She stuffs a backpack full of supplies, and then pulls out a cell phone.

"Hello, Mister Waters. This is Amy from the animal hospital.

"Yes, we're leaving soon.

"I know. Me, too."

While Amy talks, I work. She wants to know what I ate before getting sick. After everything she has done for me, I must take her to the dog. I study the map, but don't see the farm where I found the dog. No curvy road. No house. Lots of trees, but nothing else. I keep looking… Nothing, nothing, nothing… Wait! Is that a dirt road? Big barn. Lots of land. Tall oak trees. A house. Yes! It's the farmhouse!

Amy ends the call and tries putting me in a travel cage, but I make a fuss. I stomp my feet and move toward the map. "Hiss, hiss, hiss, grunt, GRUNT! *We need to stop at a FARM!*"

"I know, I know! I'm taking you to Mount Burdell!"

"Hiss, hiss, grunt, hiss, grunt! *First, I want to show you a dog!*"

Amy sighs in frustration. "I don't know what you want."

A brilliant idea suddenly pops into my mind and I move into action. I pretend to eat from my feeding bowl. Then, I open my mouth wide and act as if I am throwing up. I do this a bunch of times.

Amy rests a hand on her chin. She wears a blank expression as her eyes flit back and forth from the map to me.

Dang. She's not getting it. I need to try something else. Something more dramatic. I plop down on my back, stick out my legs, and close my eyes like I have passed out. I don't move a muscle. Then, I jump up, pretend to eat, throw up, and plop back down again.

Amy continues watching, but does not say anything.

Come on, Amy. Think! I can't keep doing this all day...

Suddenly her eyes brighten like a full moon. "Did you eat something here"—she points at the farm—"your last meal before getting sick?"

"Hissssss! Grunt, grunt, grunt! *Yesssss! You got it!*"

She smiles. "I'm guessing that's a yes?"

I continue to press on the map to make sure she understands. "Hiss, hiss, hiss! *Please drive here!*" I tap my beak up and down the road leading to the farm like I'm playing scales on a piano. Back and forth, back and forth.

"Okay, okay"—she throws her hands up in the air—"we'll

go there!"

Smart, beautiful Amy. I knew she would get it. Now, I just have to find a way to show her the dog once we arrive at the farm. That should be easy-peasy for a smart bird like me, don't you agree?

Detective Work

Amy drives north on the freeway. A few miles later we head toward the hills. We weave along a curvy road until a farmhouse comes into view. Several large oak trees and a red barn appear in the distance.

"Hiss, hiss. Hiss! *We're here. Stop!*" I grunt loudly to get her attention.

Amy screeches to a halt. "Is this the place?"

"Hiss! *Yes!*" I gaze at the farmhouse.

"I can't believe I'm actually taking directions from a turkey vulture," Amy mumbles while turning into the driveway and parking the truck. "Well, we're here. Now what?"

Returning to this place gives me the heebie-jeebies. It feels as if a hundred hairy spiders are crawling on my body. I know my mind is playing tricks on me, but it sure seems real.

I clear my brain to focus on my task. "Hiss, hiss, hiss, grunt, grunt. *I want to show you a dog.*" I stare at the two giant oak trees.

Amy follows my gaze. "You want to go over there? By those trees?"

"Hiss, hiss. *Yes, please.*"

She studies the landscape for a few minutes before saying, "OK. But first, we need to get the homeowner's permission." She hauls me up to the porch and knocks on the front door. After no one answers, she bangs harder and yells, "Hello! Is anyone home?"

An elderly man jerks the door open. "Yes? What'd ya want?" He rubs his eyes and sounds groggy, as if we woke him from a morning nap. His thin gray hair pokes out in all directions. He uses a cane to balance himself.

"Good morning, sir. My name is Amy, and I work at the animal hospital."

The man scowls at us. "What's this about?"

Amy motions toward my cage. "This vulture is my patient. She may have eaten something in your field that made her sick."

The farmer opens his mouth, but doesn't speak.

"May I look around? Perhaps I can figure out what happened," Amy says politely. "It's important that—"

"Absolutely not!" the farmer shouts, interrupting Amy and causing her to step back. "I don't know anything about a sick vulture." He frowns at me. "And that THING has no business on my property. Take it away!"

Amy and I stare at each other in shock.

"Now!" the farmer yells while using his cane to shoo us away like two pesky flies. "Get out of here before I call the cops!" He slams the door shut and disappears inside the house.

Amy stands there like a block of ice, frozen and unable to move.

Why is he so rude? I peck at the cage's door with all my might. "Hiss, hiss, hiss! *Let me out of here!*"

Amy slowly opens the door. "I'm not sure about this, but—"

I rush out and hop on the front step. I don't care if the farmer calls the cops. I am NOT leaving until Amy sees that dog. It is too important. My chest tightens as I step off the porch and stretch my wings. It's been a while since I have flown long distances, which makes me anxious. But I must do this.

I take a few steps and leap into the air expecting to fly, but fall flat on my face. *Sheesh! Talk about embarrassing...*

Amy rushes over with a worried expression. "Are you all right?"

I nod, shake dirt from my feathers, and wait for a stronger

wind gust. This time, I jump at just the right moment.

Woot-woot! I'm back in the air!

I swoop next to Amy and shout, "Hiss, hiss! *This way!*"

She walks at first, but begins sprinting to keep up.

I scan the field until I spot two tall oak trees, growing side-by-side. I land between them, but don't see the dog.

Amy finally arrives. She rests her palms on her thighs as she catches her breath. "Now what?" she asks, huffing and puffing.

I continue to search, knowing the dog is around here somewhere.

Then, I spot a mound covered by leaves and twigs. Bingo! I bet that is my last meal. "Hiss, hiss, hiss! *Check this out!*"

Amy bends over in front of the mound, brushing away leaves and dirt. "What do we have here?"

The decaying body of a black and white dog lies before us. I wish Amy understood this animal's importance. Fortunately, another brilliant idea explodes in my brain, like a firecracker on the Fourth of July.

I pretend to eat the dog and act as if I am choking. I fall to the ground in a heap of feathers.

Amy looks at me as if I have lost my mind.

I stand and repeat my performance with gusto. *Animal Planet*, here I come!

She finally smiles. A big, radiant toothy grin. "Did you eat *this* dog?" she asks excitedly. "Just before getting sick?"

Oh, yeah! I spin around, pumping my wing into the air. "HISS, HISS, HISS! *YES, YES, YES!*" I am so happy I jump for joy.

"It's time we have another conversation with the farmer." Amy slips on gloves, scoops up the dog, and puts it in a black plastic bag. She flings it over her shoulder. "You ready?"

I nod briskly. "Hiss, hiss! *Let's roll!*"

Doing the Right Thing

We return to the farmhouse. Amy knocks on the door, but the farmer doesn't answer. She knocks again—much louder—while tapping her foot rapidly.

My eyes drift toward the plastic bag, and my tummy does a back flip. It feels as if I ate that dog again even though I didn't. Isn't that strange?

Amy glances at me. "Don't worry. We're not leaving here until I get some answers." She pounds on the door a third time as if she is trying to break it down.

Finally, we hear footsteps—shuffle, shuffle, shuffle—and the door pops open. The farmer yells, "I told you to leave!"

Amy ignores his tone and raises the bag. "I found"—she winks at me—"we found this dog in your field. May I ask you a few questions?"

Just then, a car rolls into the driveway. The farmer points his cane at it. "That's my wife. I want you to leave before you upset her with this silly nonsense!"

A plump, gray haired lady walks up carrying a bag of groceries. "Good morning," she says pleasantly. "I'm Claire."

Claire's green eyes glisten like a handful of soap bubbles. She squats in front of me as if we are best buddies.

"And whom do we have here?" she asks warmly.

"Hiss, hiss, hiss, grunt! Hiss, grunt, grunt, grunt. *Please listen to Amy! She has something important to say.*"

Claire nearly falls over. "Well, I'll be. Never heard a turkey

vulture talk before."

Amy stands next to Claire. "I'm a vet at the animal hospital, and this vulture is my patient."

Claire nods and listens.

"She ate something that poisoned her"—Amy lifts the bag —"and this may be it."

The farmer's face reddens as he moves closer to us. "Now wait just a minute! You can't come here and—"

Claire touches the farmer's arm gently. "Now honey, let's hear what she has to say."

"But I—"

"Please, James. Give her a chance to speak."

James folds his arms and pouts like a two-year-old throwing a temper tantrum. His behavior cracks me up, but I don't laugh. I need to focus and be serious right now.

Amy tells Claire my story, and then says, "May I ask you a couple of important questions?"

"Of course, dear." Claire sets the groceries on a table. "How can I help?"

Amy unties the plastic bag. "Do you recognize this animal?"

Claire peaks inside and gasps loudly, pressing her hand against her chest. "Oh, dear. It looks like Sophie. My dog." She glances at her husband. "James buried her after the vet left our house." She pauses while looking at the bag. "Sophie died a few weeks ago."

"I'm sorry for your loss," Amy says respectfully.

Claire searches for a tissue inside her purse while asking, "Why is our dog in that bag?"

Amy explains how we found the body in the field. She asks, "Did the vet give Sophie medicine to help her...go to sleep?"

"Why, yes. We didn't want her to suffer." Claire wipes away a tear. "She was very sick."

Amy gives Claire a moment to calm herself, and then asks, "Do you remember the name of the drug?"

"I, uh…" Claire shrugs. "I don't know. I'm sorry."

James mumbles, "I'll get the paperwork." He walks inside the house and returns a few minutes later. He presses a paper in Amy's hand. "This is what the vet gave us."

Amy reads slowly, soaking in every word. Afterward, she sighs and shakes her head. "Sophie was given the same drug we found inside the vulture."

James removes a handkerchief from his pocket and wipes his forehead. "But I buried my dog properly," he explains. "I covered her up. Completely."

Amy nods. "I'm sure you did. But something dug her up, and this vulture found her."

James stares at me. "Did you…did you eat our Sophie?"

I lower my head, wondering how to respond. *Doesn't he know that vultures feed on dead animals? Shall I tell him about Rosie being hungry?* I end up not saying anything. I ate their beloved pet and feel ashamed.

Amy rubs my back. "My little friend was only doing her job. She keeps the environment free from disease by eating rotting animals."

"I understand," Claire says.

"Unfortunately, when she ate Sophie, she also ate the drug. That's what made her sick. It's called secondary poisoning," Amy explains. "She almost died."

"Oh, dear," Claire says, looking concerned.

Amy continues, "The vulture guided me here. She wants to prevent other animals from getting sick."

"What a thoughtful thing to do," Claire says.

I lower my head as my face warms. Getting all this attention is uncomfortable. But I cannot lie. I enjoy the compliments.

Amy asks James and Claire, "Shall we work together to bury Sophie? We'll make sure nothing digs her up this time."

"That would be kind of you, dear." Claire turns toward me. "I'm sorry my dog made you sick."

"Hiss, hiss. Grunt, grunt, hiss. *It's OK. I'm better now.*"

Claire asks Amy, "Do you know what the vulture said?"

"I'm not sure. But she seems happy."

Claire nods. "She's one-of-a-kind, that's for sure."

James clears his throat, "I'll get a shovel." He limps toward the barn.

Amy nods while removing a cell phone from her backpack. *Who is she calling now?*

A Proper Burial

Amy, James, Claire and I return to the oak trees where we found Sophie. This time, James digs a larger, and much deeper, hole with Amy's help. Claire carefully lays Sophie's body in it. James replaces the dirt and firmly pats the ground with the shovel. Amy gathers several baseball-size rocks, and places them on top of the grave. She makes sure nothing will ever bother Sophie again.

"Our Sophie can finally be at peace," Claire says. She bends down beside me. "Thanks for bringing Amy here. You are very brave."

I bounce up and down, feeling thrilled about how everything is turning out. "Hiss, hiss, grunt. *I'm glad to help.*"

"My, my. You have such a friendly personality!" Claire says. "I hope you come back and visit us."

Before I can respond, Amy asks Claire and James, "Would you like to do something fun with me?"

"What do you have in mind, dear?"

Amy looks my way, and soon, so do Claire and James.

Why are they all staring?

Return to the Wild

Amy brushes dirt off her hands and gestures toward a field. "Will everyone please follow me?"

James and Claire leave right away, but I take another minute with the dog. She had a good life with her family. They loved her. "Hiss, hiss. Hiss, hiss, grunt. *So long, Sophie. I'm sorry I disturbed you.*" Knowing she is safe now, I hop away to join the others.

We arrive at the field, and Amy glances at her watch. Soon, a car drives up, and an older man and young girl walk toward us.

Amy strolls over to greet them. "Mister Waters?"

He takes off a Greek Fisherman's hat and nods. "That's me. But you can call me Andy. And this is Ruby, my granddaughter."

"Nice to meet you both." Amy shakes their hands. "I'm glad

you could join us."

Something about the man's hat and the girl's smile looks familiar. All of a sudden, it hits me like a ton of bricks. It's the birdfeeders! They helped me after I crashed in their backyard.

"So…this is our vulture?" Andy says.

Ruby hops from foot to foot. "Oh, Papa, I KNOW it's her! Check out that purple sheen! I'd recognize it anywhere!"

Papa and Ruby. My rescuers. I move toward them. "Hiss, hiss, hiss, grunt, grunt. *I wouldn't be alive without your help.*"

Ruby leaps behind her grandfather, but slowly sticks her head out. "What'd she say, Papa?"

"I'm not sure, but she seems excited to see us."

Why did Ruby hide behind her grandfather? By now, she must know I would never hurt her. And Papa is correct. I am excited to see them. We are friends!

Amy motions for everyone to gather around her. "This little vulture has touched all of our lives. She has worked hard to regain her health. Now, she is ready to return home. Thank you for joining me as we release her back into the wild."

Ahhh…Now, I get what is happening. Papa, Ruby, Claire and James have each helped in their own way, but Amy and I have formed a special bond. Even though I don't want to leave her, I must. It is the way of nature.

Before returning home, I need one more thing from Amy. I want her to say my name. Not '1474' or 'little friend or 'little girl' or 'little vulture.' I want her to say 'Vanessa.' If she does, we will be linked forever.

How can I make it happen?

I search the area and see two sticks, which triggers a crafty idea. I move the sticks together to form a "V." Next I gather pieces of tall grass and shape it into an "A." I keep going—finding twigs, rocks, flowers, plants—until I spell out my name. I stand back and wait.

Amy sounds out each letter slowly—V A N E S S A—before saying, "Vanessa?" Her mouth drops open and she asks, "Is that your name?"

"Hiss, hiss, hiss! *You got it!*" Hearing her say it makes my body tingle.

"It's a lovely name." Amy brushes away a tear. "You are an inspiration, Vanessa, and I will miss you. I am so glad we met."

I know if I don't leave now, I never will. I take a few steps, but turn around. All five humans are watching me.

"Go ahead, Vanessa." Amy gently nudges. "It's time to go home."

I search for a launching pad, and find a big log. I hop on it, spread my wings, and fan my tail. When a proper wind gust arrives, I jump into it.

I circle above Amy, James, Claire, Papa and Ruby, tipping

my wing in a farewell salute. Soon, they become tiny specks of waving hands before disappearing from sight.

As I fly home, my heart races with uncertainty. I have been gone for so long. *Will my family remember me?*

Going Home

I soar across wide stretches of land. Hikers, dogs, and runners appear on trails below. Children's voices from a park float through the air. I fly over trees and creeks and hills until I find the familiar path leading home.

I wonder how Rosie is doing? Will Momma be angry at me for leaving her?

My tummy does a cartwheel when I see vultures roosting in our family tree. My heart flutters as their faces become clear. Uncle Kenny and Aunt Betty, cousins Camden and Bobby. And Rosie! There's Jason! He is bigger than I remember. And there's my mom and dad!

I am shaking as I land on the first empty branch. Everyone stares as if I'm a stranger. My mother's eyes sparkle in the afternoon sunlight. Oh, how I have missed her.

"Hiss! Hiss! Grunt, hiss! Grunt! *Momma! Momma! It's me! Vanessa!*" I tremble with excitement. "Hissssssss! Grunt, grunt! *Mommaaaaa! I'm home!*"

At first she doesn't move. She seems frightened, as if I am a ghost. Then, she smiles. A dazzling smile that makes my heart burst with love.

She hugs me tenderly, and I feel loved. "My little girl"— she steps back and gazes at me—"is it really you?"

The entire family gathers around, kissing and hugging me for a long time. Then, questions start flying left and right:

"What happened to you?"

"Where have you been?"

"Why didn't you come home?"

"Did you get hurt?"

"Are you all right?"

I describe everything that took place after I left home. I apologize for leaving Rosie alone, but it doesn't seem to matter now. All Momma and Daddy care about is having me home. I tell them how kindly the humans have treated me—especially Amy.

Rosie pushes her way to the front. She wraps her wings

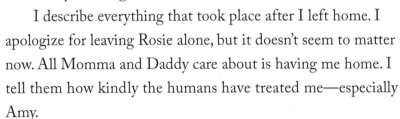

around my neck, causing me to gasp for air. "I was so worried when you didn't return!" She flaps her wings several times. "I'm all better now. Wanna play tag?" She giggles and touches my head, "You're it!"

It is nice to know some things never change, and Rosie didn't starve while I was away. My family surrounds me, and I know one thing for sure: there is no place like home.

A Perfect Day

The next morning, I wake up huddled next to my parents and Jason in our family tree. I have never felt so happy.

"Good morning, sweetheart," Momma says. "Did you sleep well?"

Before I can respond, my dad asks, "How are you this morning?"

I yawn and stretch my wings. "I feel w-o-n-d-e-r-f-u-l!"

Jason playfully wing-bumps me. "Did you miss me, little sister?"

I toss him a 'don't mess with me' look, and he laughs. He is still the same Jason, and I wouldn't change him for anything. I love my twin brother.

"I bet you're hungry, Vanessa," Momma says. "Shall we

hunt for food?"

"Maybe she should take it easy, Mom," Jason says while grinning. "She's been through a lot."

I know he is teasing, so I ignore the comment. "I'd love to hunt with you, Momma." I spread my wings so the sun can dry them.

I bounce up and down a few times to warm my legs. When the time is right, I jump into a gust of wind. I shout over my shoulder, "What are you waiting for?"

Soon everyone—including Rosie—joins me in the air. I wait for my dad to take the lead. He soars north toward our usual hunting area, but surprises us by turning south. Everyone follows.

I drift next to him and ask, "Where are we headed, Daddy?"

"It's a surprise," he says. "Somewhere special."

We follow the freeway, soaring across several shopping malls, over apartment buildings and houses, by mountains and trails. When tall trees appear in the distance, a shiver runs down my spine. I can barely fly straight.

After a few more miles, I see them up close. The coastal redwoods. The tallest tree in the world. I soar around them, beside them, and above them before settling on a high branch. I am completely lost in the moment's joy. The trees are magnificent! A hundred times better than I ever imagined in my mind.

The wind whistles a lovely tune as it pushes through the forest. Sitting here is awesome, like watching a colorful sunset with someone you love.

Jason swoops in and perches next to me. "Do you know where we are, Vanessa?"

The trees are huge and almost touch the sky. They make humans look like ants. "This is Muir Woods, isn't it?"

"Uh-huh. I told you it was amazing." Jason nestles closer. "I'm glad you're home, Sis. Things weren't the same without you. I missed you."

I snuggle closer to Jason just as my tummy gurgles.

He chuckles. "I know what that sound means. Follow me." He leaps from the tree and guides us through the forest. We circle in the air until we spot a dead deer lying in the brush. We land on the ground, and Jason pats his stomach. "Our lucky day."

We approach the deer and see no danger, so we take our first bite. The food tastes delicious. The rest of my family soon joins us for breakfast.

As I look around at my loved ones and Muir Woods, I feel content. Today is the best day of my life. It's like having my birthday, Halloween and summer vacation all rolled up into one perfect day. A girl couldn't ask for more.

And that, my friends, is the end of this incredible true story. I hope you enjoyed it. Oh, and by the way, the next time you see a turkey vulture circling overhead or standing by the roadside, please wave. It just might be…

Your new BEST friend,
Vanessa T. Vulture

AUTHORS' NOTES

Vanessa's Rotten Day is based on a true animal rescue story. In July 2014, we found this vulture lying comatose in our backyard and called the Humane Society. An animal rescue worker scooped up the bird and rushed her to *WildCare* in San Rafael.

Melanie Piazza, Director of Animal Care at *WildCare*, and her dedicated team of volunteers worked tirelessly to save Vanessa's life. While we took significant creative liberties in writing this story, the medical procedures described in the book were actually performed on the vulture. Three weeks after this photograph was taken, Melanie released a healthy vulture back into the wild—the goal for all rescued animals.

California Department of Fish and Wildlife officials confirmed that from July to October 2014, six turkey vultures who were treated at *WildCare* had been poisoned. A drug called pentobarbital was found inside of them. The medicine is used by veterinarians to euthanize unhealthy animals such as dogs, livestock, and horses. A seventh vulture nearly died after eating a rat that had been poisoned.

Most people do not intentionally harm wildlife. But sadly,

that is exactly what happens when euthanized animals are not buried properly, or when people use poison, instead of traps, to kill rats.

According to *WildCare* experts, turkey vultures are important to the ecosystem, essentially serving as nature's trash collectors for animals that die in the wild. Vultures have a highly developed sense of smell, and their digestive system is capable of killing any viruses or bacteria they eat. They are protected by the Federal Migratory Bird Treaty Act of 1918 and California Fish and Game Code.

We hope you found our story entertaining as well as educational. Please join us in spreading the word about how to prevent secondary poisoning.

Best wishes,
Roberta & Collette
www.robertacarr.com

ACKNOWLEDGMENTS

Melanie Piazza is the director of Animal Care at *WildCare* in San Rafael. She is a skilled animal rehabilitator, and we thank her for the behind-the-scenes tour, and for educating us about the diagnosis, treatment, and recovery goals of animals who are victims of secondary poisoning.

Andrew C. Carr is an avid bird photographer. He scoured Novato to find vultures to photograph for us. He took many remarkable pictures that inspired the illustrator in her work. Andy was also an early reader of the manuscript, providing valuable feedback.

We are grateful to **Debora Strand** for stepping out of her comfort zone to tackle the vulture illustrations. She is a gifted watercolorist who brought Vanessa to life. Our friend **Sandy** provided input on the illustrations.

Debra Toor's book, *Survival Secrets of Turkey Vultures*, educated us about these amazing creatures. Debra's research and images helped us add a touch of realism to our whimsical story.

Alison Hermance and **Megan Hansen** wrote articles for local Marin newspapers about our vulture's ordeal. Their facts served as source material for this story.

Thanks to **Adam, Camden, Debora, Gaye** and **Kimberly** for being early readers. Each of them offered helpful feedback that improved the manuscript.

We appreciate **Carol Callahan** for editing, formatting the book, and designing the cover layout.

We are grateful to the Marin Humane Society for responding so quickly to our emergency call. You helped save Vanessa's life.

Last, but not least, we thank the friendly staff at the *Double Rainbow Café* in San Rafael for never chasing the authors out of our favorite booth as we plotted and wrote the story over many months.

ABOUT THE AUTHORS

Roberta R. Carr lives in Novato, California. She had an enjoyable career in health care before leaving to become a full-time writer. She helped her husband write his Vietnam War memoir, and has self-published three novels: *The Vernazza Effect* (2013), *The Foundation* (2014), and *The Bennett Women* (2015). Collaborating with her granddaughter to write *Vanessa's Rotten Day* was a labor of love. Currently, she is working on a sequel to *The Bennett Women*. To read more about her work, please visit her website: www.robertacarr.com.

Collette Treewater is an energetic fourth-grader at Glenwood Elementary School in San Rafael, California. She enjoys math, science, and writing. Gymnastics is her favorite sport. She adores looming, and has completed many creative projects. She likes having her grandmother pick her up after school every Wednesday. They often hang out at *Double Rainbow Café* to eat ice cream and talk about all kinds of things. Collette loves having her Golden Retriever, Ruby, greet her at the end of a busy day.

Made in the USA
San Bernardino, CA
17 March 2019